TOOLS FOR TEACHERS

- **ATOS:** 0.9
- **GRL:** D
- **WORD COUNT:** 46

- **CURRICULUM CONNECTIONS:**
  community helpers,
  law enforcement

Skills to Teach

- **HIGH-FREQUENCY WORDS:** a, an, go, is, the, to, us
- **CONTENT WORDS:** car, child, crashed, crime, dog, finds, helps, lost, police, officers, safe, station, works
- **PUNCTUATION:** periods, exclamation points, apostrophe, question mark, comma
- **WORD STUDY:** /s/, spelled c (*place, police, officers*); /sh/, spelled *ti* (*station*)
- **TEXT TYPE:** factual description

Before Reading Activities

- Read the title and give a simple statement of the main idea.
- Have students "walk" though the book and talk about what they see in the pictures.
- Introduce new vocabulary by having students predict the first letter and locate the word in the text.
- Discuss any unfamiliar concepts that are in the text.

After Reading Activities

Encourage children to talk about their experiences with police officers. Have they ever met a police officer? Have they seen police officers depicted on television? Does knowing what police officers do to protect the public help them feel safer?

Tadpole Books are published by Jump!, 5357 Penn Avenue South, Minneapolis, MN 55419, www.jumplibrary.com

Copyright ©2018 Jump! International copyright reserved in all countries. No part of this book may be reproduced in any form without written permission from the publisher.

Editorial: Hundred Acre Words, LLC **Designer:** Anna Peterson

Photo Credits: Alamy: Jeff Gilbert, 4–5. Getty: Richard Hutchings, 8–9. iStock: lovleah, 10–11. Shutterstock: Creativa Images, 6–7; Dani Simmonds, 1; Darren Brode, 16; Fotokon, 2–3; hans engbers, cover; iofoto, 6–7; Monika Wisniewska, 12–13; Nerthuz, cover.

Library of Congress Cataloging-in-Publication Data
Names: Donner, Erica, author.
Title: Police station / by Erica Donner.
Description: Minneapolis: Jump!, Inc., (2017) | Series: Around town | Includes index.
Identifiers: LCCN 2017034013 (print) | LCCN 2017034485 (ebook) | ISBN 9781624967146 (ebook) | ISBN 9781620319314 (hardcover: alk. paper) | ISBN 9781620319321 (pbk.)
Subjects: LCSH: Police—Juvenile literature. | Police stations—Juvenile literature.
Classification: LCC HV7922 (ebook) | LCC HV7922 .D66 2017 (print) | DDC 363.2/3—dc23
LC record available at https://lccn.loc.gov/2017034013

AROUND TOWN

POLICE STATION

by Erica Donner

TABLE OF CONTENTS

tadpole
books

POLICE STATION

Let's go to the
police station.

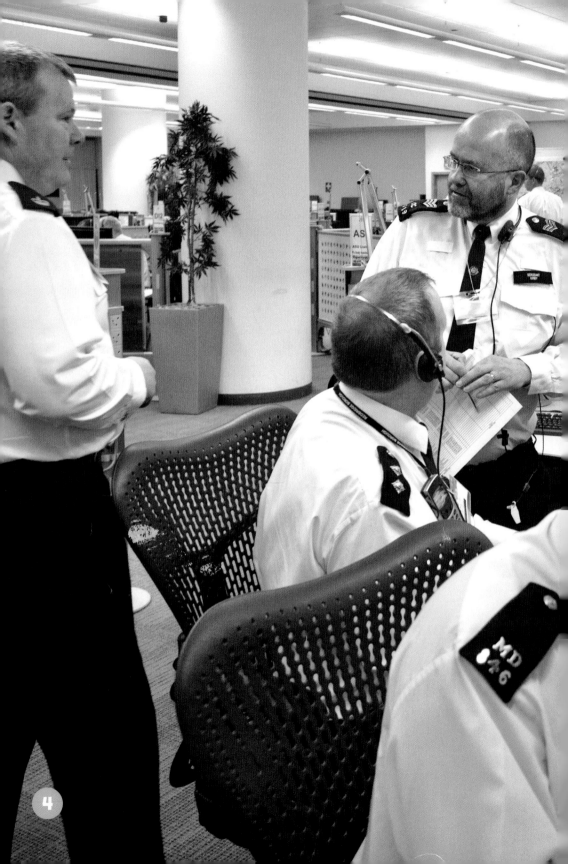

Who works here? Police officers.

A car crashed.
An officer helps.

A child is lost.
An officer helps.

A crime took place. An officer helps.

**A dog helps, too.
He finds things.**

Police officers help keep us safe!

WORDS TO KNOW

car

child

crashed

dog

police officers

police station

INDEX